NIGHT-TIME STORIES

AF004926

OTHER TITLES FROM THE EMMA PRESS

SHORT STORIES AND ESSAYS

Hailman, by Leanne Radojkovich
Postcard Stories 2, by Jan Carson
Tiny Moons, by Nina Mingya Powles
Once Upon A Time In Birmingham, by Louise Palfreyman
The Secret Box, by Daina Tabūna, tr. from Latvian by Jayde Will

POETRY COLLECTIONS

Europe, Love Me Back, by Rakhshan Rizwan

POETRY AND ART SQUARES

Menagerie, by Cheryl Pearson, illus. by Amy Louise Evans
One day at the Taiwan Land Bank Dinosaur Museum, by Elīna Eihmane
Pilgrim, by Lisabelle Tay, illus. by Reena Makwana
The Fox's Wedding, by Rebecca Hurst, illus. by Reena Makwana

POETRY PAMPHLETS

The Fabulanarchist Luxury Uprising, by Jack Houston
The Bell Tower, by Pamela Crowe
Ovarium, by Joanna Ingham
Milk Snake, by Toby Buckley

BOOKS FOR CHILDREN

Poems the wind blew in, by Karmelo C Iribarren,
tr. from Spanish by Lawrence Schimel
My Sneezes Are Perfect, by Rakhshan Rizwan
The Bee Is Not Afraid of Me: A Book of Insect Poems,
edited by Fran Long and Isabel Galleymore
Cloud Soup, by Kate Wakeling

NIGHT-TIME STORIES

EDITED BY
Yen-Yen Lu

WITH STORIES FROM
Valentine Carter, John Kitchen,
Winifred Mok, Leanne Radojkovich,
Angela Readman, Jane Roberts,
Rebecca Rouillard, Miyuki Tatsuma,
Zoë Wells and Sofija Ana Zovko

| ιι|ι ιιιιιι

THE EMMA PRESS

First published in the UK in 2022 by The Emma Press Ltd.

Stories © individual writers 2022
Selection and introduction © Yen-Yen Lu 2022

All rights reserved.

The rights of Yen-Yen Lu to be identified as the editor of this anthology and the writers to be identified as the authors of their stories have been asserted in accordance with the Copyright, Designs and Patents Act 1988.

ISBN 978-1-912915-60-6

A CIP catalogue record of this book
is available from the British Library.

Printed and bound in the UK
by TJ Books, Padstow.

The Emma Press
theemmapress.com
hello@theemmapress.com
Birmingham, UK

Introduction from the editor

Once, when I was fourteen, I stayed up for an entire night. It wasn't planned and I didn't do anything or go anywhere particularly exciting: I sat on my bedroom floor, I read, I listened to the radio. All things I might do in the daytime, but there was something thrilling about doing them at night.

I've since experienced many nights that were objectively more eventful and exciting, a few involving ghosts and/or alcohol, but I always come back to this night. The quiet electricity in the air as I sat with my book. My hope as I began editing this anthology was to find stories that capture the strangeness and subtle magic that I experienced that night, that I've experienced since, and that many others share, judging by the number of submissions we received for the theme.

It was also important for me to choose a universal theme for The Emma Press' first short story anthology, as I hoped to encourage a greater range of writers to submit their work and explore what a night-time story meant to them.

As a result, this anthology encapsulates a spectrum of night-time stories, from intense and surreal to wonderfully mundane.

There is some literal magic and fantasy in these stories, which I expected and looked forward to while reading submissions. A beautiful example features in John Kitchen's 'dream lovers', where acquaintances develop a closer and more intimate relationship through shared dreams. And in 'Kikimora' by Sofija Ana Zovko, a woman learns that a mischievous creature she believed to be a figment of her late grandmother's imagination comes to life at night. These stories reminded me of how, sometimes, the mystical connections that you might be sceptical about during the day can seem much more believable after dark.

Other stories explore more everyday activities and find magic in the mundane. A quiet supermarket trip in 'Even This Helps' by Zoë Wells magnifies even the smallest moments into something more mysterious than they really are. A similar concept runs through 'Sleeping in Shifts' by Winifred Mok, where filmmakers living in close quarters observe the differences in working a day shift and a night shift, as well as the differences between a 'day person' and a 'night person'. Parts of these stories resonated with me and made me think again of staying up all night when I was a teenager, noticing how eerie and quiet the world seemed.

Many of the stories in the anthology explore the idea that, in contrast to a fast-paced daytime atmosphere, the night is a time to slow down and reflect, but it's necessary to have both light and dark to appreciate the other. This feels particularly important in a year of so much uncertainty – at the same time, while plans are put on hold, many are finding an opportunity to slow down and pay attention to quieter, more peaceful moments.

It was a joy to put this anthology together and to have collected stories that, although they share a similar theme, draw on unique cultures and customs from all over the world, from across the UK to New Zealand to Poland. I hope that readers might find something familiar in this anthology and enjoy reading them as much as I did.

Yen-Yen Lu, November 2020

CONTENTS

Introduction from the editor V

The Girls are Pretty Crocodiles Now,
by Angela Readman 1

Sleeping in Shifts, by Winifred Mok 5

Whose Lounge? by Leanne Radojkovich 9

Obon, by Miyuki Tatsuma 13

Dream Boats, by Jane Roberts 19

(hippocampus paradoxus), by Valentine Carter ... 21

Daylight Saving Time, by Rebecca Rouillard 27

Kikimora, by Sofija Ana Zovko 37

dream lovers, by John Kitchen 49

Even This Helps, by Zoë Wells 51

About the writers 57
About the editor 60
About The Emma Press 61

The Girls are Pretty Crocodiles Now

| ١١١ ١١١١١

Angela Readman

Lately, I look out of the window at night and always see some girl just like me looking out in her pyjamas, fingers pressed to her cheek. The streets glow with night-lights; none of us can sleep. It's been like this since Jonah claimed he caught the tooth fairy.

He was sucking a gobstopper when he told me, the kind with as many layers as a planet. Every so often he spat it onto his palm to see if it had changed colour, like a mood ring of his big fat mouth.

'You want a lick?' he asked. The gobstopper was purple, except around his fingers where it was red. I shook my head and pushed a loose canine back and forth with my tongue. It was taking so long to come out I'd developed a mannerism of pushing my tongue to the side of my face constantly.

'You won't get anything, you know, when that tooth falls out. There's no fairy. Not anymore.'

'I know there's not,' I said, 'but I'll still get a quid. My mam will put it there.'

I felt awful then because Jonah's mother was gone. I didn't feel it a second later. Jonah was the sort of kid whose face looked so gleeful breaking bad news, no one could care about him for long.

'I'll show you,' he said. 'Come with me.'

I followed him along the terrace and up to his room. I'd never been in his house before. It smelt like the dentist's combined with Cup-a-Soup and old car manuals. The white coat his mother used to wear for work hung on the back of his bedroom door. I wondered if he put it on sometimes. Or if there was a moment, when he crawled into bed at night, he could imagine her walking in.

'Look.' Jonah handed me a beetroot jar. I held it to the light. There was nothing inside but a set of small wings and smudges on the glass.

The wings reminded me of dragonflies I'd sometimes find on the windowsill in October, like stained glass with no daylight to catch them. Yet if I held them up to the lamp, I could picture a river. I always kept them on my ledge like a slither of summer until they eventually became nothing but a layer of powder on the paint.

'It's just an insect,' I said. 'That's all you killed. Anyone can do that.'

Jonah grinned. 'Really? Think what you like. No skin off my nose.'

I looked at the jar, holding it so close I could feel my eyelashes against it. There was something off about it, something I'd never seen with a caught insect. Footprints. All over the jar were tiny marks like someone had been pacing. There were dusty grids on the glass like a boot had kicked and kicked, wanting out. Looking at the small raspberry-coloured smears, they reminded me of fists.

'Shitehawk.' I shoved the jar at Jonah and left him crunching into the bubble gum in the centre of his gobstopper. I didn't believe him, but I kept picturing the jar. Something small and breathing inside it like a spider caught under a vase, playing dead and lurching whenever someone opened it a chink.

I wiggled my tooth back and forth all the next day, watching Jonah telling some other girl what he had done and producing the jar from his pocket.

I don't believe you, I don't believe you, I heard girls say, peering in. We all refused a lick of his slimy gobstopper and stormed off, milk teeth wiggling in our mouths.

I can't stop noticing how our proper teeth keep coming in now, yet our baby teeth flat refuse to fall out. It's as if, without knowing we'll get something in return, a girl can't let anything go. I look around at girls with smiles like pretty crocodiles. All day we grin and claim boys are liars. We close our doors, pick up our toothbrushes and go to bed minty fresh. All night, our tongues push at loose teeth like pearl doors. We picture wings and bloody fists as we put on our night lights and peer outside and see girls who can't sleep all along the street. Looking up, crane flies crackle like dangerous wiring, a soft beat of moths stunning themselves on the streetlights. Believing nothing, one by one, we reach out and open our windows in case something wants to fly in.

Sleeping in Shifts

Winifred Mok

I live with a night person.

I'm not strictly a 'day person' – early mornings are not my thing – but I'm drawn to the sun. I get cold easily; I don't like the dark. When you've travelled around, you notice that the sun shines in different tones, colours, and densities. In England, it's a backseat observer, gazing through clouds onto rolling greens. In Southern Africa, it's a heavy beast, omnipresent, close enough to smell; the dust is heavy with it. And at home, in South East Asia, it's like a parent: temperamental, mostly overbearing. The heat waves seek you through the concrete jungle, insulated by layers upon layers of high rises, through street stalls and in large malls. Though we strive to adapt to different circumstances, different climates, the warmth of daybreak has always been my natural alarm.

I wake to a clicking mouse, a clacking keyboard. In this house, it's just the two of us; these days we exist in different time zones within the same space. As I rise, called by daylight, he shows me the progress he's made.

It's 10am when he crawls off into the depths of blankets and I take on the baton. We are filmmakers and we are currently in the limbo of post-production. He's finished the rough cut, and leaves me with the next job of sound editing. Even without breakfast, my mind is already working. 18-hour days are the norm here, at least until the job's done. Thus is the life of those who work at home, or live at work.

It's just me and the screen.

Though the rays of sun stream through the curtains, he slumbers deeply in the quiet of the living day. My work begins with cleaning: not unlike housework, the background dust of the video is swept with some noise reduction, whilst EQ filters help purify and clarify. Sometimes, when there's a pop, a click, an unwanted blip, I use my mouse to scrub it away. These are all private noises; I travel forth in search of normalisation, in search of balance – as the room stays silent.

There are various channels to consider: voice, music, room tone. The scenes play through the headphones and my ears are filled with story and characters. Sound editing requires trimming, transitions, long fades and cuts. As they say, *you win some, you lose some:* audio balancing involves gain (volume) and loss (compression), avoiding those mountainous peaks (clipping), and arriving at the perfect mix of anticipation and excitement. The shaping of the narrative is a narrative in itself.

Immersed in a fictitious reality, I find myself losing time, losing light, and as my teacup reaches its nth cup of chai, it's time for food. It's difficult to sync, to think, what to prepare: dinner for me, breakfast for him?

He seems to sense when night has arrived; he rises with the moon. We have a little time in this gap – his dawn, my twilight. Our timelines cross briefly, like a lunar eclipse.

I'm almost done with the sound; he'll be fixing the colour next. The vivid shades will fade from the sky while he intensifies cinematic hues and saturation on the colour wheels. He says he prefers the night; the truth comes out in the nocturnal morning. All is bared: all the reality and all the ugliness, the junk backstage that hasn't been cleared after the performance. The restocking of shelves, the cleaning of streets. There's nowhere to hide when all you have are shadows.

In the dead of night is a world without that sunshine-rosy-glasses-glow; a different kind of life (happily) unknown to night-sleepers. The noises of these forests are not your usual sing-along songs, as we pass our 'days' through to the small hours. When you know there is a dark side to the moon, that crescent blade of light becomes multi-dimensional.

We juxtapose images on the screen for such effect. Our work in fiction is not so different from the truth.

Soon, it'll be just him, and the screen.

Whose Lounge?

Leanne Radojkovich

'What happens when no-one is the lounge?' my daughter asked.

'Nothing.'

'Does the furniture move around?'

'No, nothing moves. Nothing happens.'

'What happens when nothing happens?'

'Don't be silly.'

'How do you know nothing happens?'

'I just do.'

'But how?'

'Stop asking, it's late. I'm tired.'

The question continued circling, mutely, until she went to bed.

After tucking her in, I went back into the lounge and sat on the sofa. I watched a fly stagger up the lampshade.

I'll *film* nothing, I thought. I put my camera on a tripod at the back of the room, left the table lamp on, and pressed record.

The next day, after dinner, I asked my daughter if she'd like to see what happened when no-one was in the lounge the night before, as I'd recorded it. 'Yes!' She jumped down off her chair and raced into the lounge. 'Put it on! Put it on!' We snuggled on the sofa to watch.

The table lamp made a pool of creamy light on screen, softening the edges of the sofa, the coffee table, and the television. It was weird seeing a smaller version of our television, nested inside our television.

We watched nothing happen for a while.

'Boring,' my daughter whined. She stomped off to her room.

I was a bit bored as well – yet intrigued at how difficult it was to tell if time was passing while watching this static image of our lounge within our lounge. Then a shimmer crossed the filmed curtains as car lights passed. A pale dot floated from the curtains – a moth. It fluttered across to the table, landing on the lamp where it became a shadow like a smut on a silver spoon. I thought I heard a dog bark off screen. A whoosh of raindrops too. I'd nearly dozed off when the cat came into view. She spent ages rubbing her face on the edge of the sofa, rubbing her face on the edge of the coffee table, and crossing to the television to rub her face against the cabinet.

There was a burst of noise as a car backfired – the cat pointed toward the sound, tail erect, head forward. There was something reptilian about her profile that I hadn't noticed before. Ears flattened and neck elongated, she had a similar silhouette to a snake. The car vroomed away and she turned to face the camera. Her eyes glowed weirdly – no pupils. Which seemed to make her head grow.

Then she did the face-rubbing rounds again: sofa, coffee table, television cabinet. All her face-rubs built up a smell-shape like a blob of clay thrown onto a potter's wheel, thinning upwards into a pot.

I felt myself becoming a little less substantial as I watched.

The cat sat on the carpet and began purring.

A swish of rain against the windows.

The moth-smut gracefully lifted up off the lampshade, turning into a shimmer again.

The cat sprang into the air. Caught the moth in her jaws. Released it onto the carpet – a motionless smudge. The cat pushed it around, but it didn't respond. She crouched beside it and yawned, reptilian again – her flip-top head.

Purring.

Rain.

Eventually, the curtains lightened with dawn.

The screen went black.

I felt so calm. More moth or cat or curtain than single mum, expected to know everything.

Obon

Miyuki Tatsuma

Obaachan had taken up salsa dancing at the age of seventy-five. One evening, when we were visiting her in her Saitama home, she taught me the basics. To my dismay, my body was devoid of any dancer's grace whatsoever, and I was tripping on my own feet.

'Take a step backwards,' she explained gently, 'and bring it back – then, with your other foot, step forwards – and back again.'

She put on her favourite Latin dance instrumental CD and I watched her sway her hips. Her eyes were overcome with a haze, separating her from this world – before I knew it, she was dancing on the wind, above the rooftops of her neighbourhood, floating towards some bright hall in Ginza full of sleek gentlemen and elegant ladies where, at heart, she had always belonged.

'You know, Ojichan would never even let me go out to buy a new dress,' she said, with a slight giggle.

I shot a glance towards the small shrine in the corner of the room, where a thin trail of smoke coiled patiently upwards from the incense. It was bad to speak ill of the departed, particularly on an August night. A shiver went through me as I realised Obaachan's joking tone hid something much darker and deeper, a sunken continent of memory better left undisturbed. But she danced on, as if the stifling heat of the evening and intoxicating incense had no sway over her. A thwarted Cinderella, who had found her way to blossom at last.

As usual, I couldn't sleep at night. My mum, my sister and I stayed upstairs, in Obaachan and Ojichan's old bedroom. Whether it was the temperature or something else, I felt restless and kept turning on the sweaty futon. Obon was a liminal time in Japan – a week in the hottest summer month when spirits of the dead came back to earth. During the hours of insomnia, I frequently lay awake all night battling my own self in trying not to think too much. As if, by staying awake, I inflated and held in place a protective membrane around my family against Time. But what could I, a feeble young thing, do against life itself? I couldn't endure the sensation of something scratching from the inside, trying to break out from my body. I sat up and contemplated the room in the bluish moonlight coming through the open balcony door. I felt the seconds, minutes, hours slashing immaterially at my skin, and my mother's and sister's – and there was nothing to be done to stop it.

The itch inside was getting intolerable, forcing me to stand up. I tried to step as quietly as I could on the tatami mats on the floor. As I turned to the balcony, I was acutely aware of the room behind me – the sliding paper doors concealed a wardrobe, where Obaachan kept Ojichan's old clothes. The room was still; but behind the steady breathing of my mother and sister I knew the shadows were stirring. I stepped barefoot onto the warm panels of the balcony. The air was sultry, and the metallic cries of the cicada cut through the silent night. What would happen to this house in fifty years' time? Obaachan's lovely garden and all her dainty things, and her dresses. I wished I could do something to protect it – get rich and hire someone to watch over it when we were away. My own future, however – my biggest fear – stared right at me; the whole night sky seemed to become it, a monstrous, gaping hollow face.

Useless, all was useless; I wanted to jump. I looked down and saw the nocturnal ghosts crowding below and behind me. Beckoning. I tried desperately to harness any remaining sense of my own corporeality before it was eaten up by the dark. I raised my hands into the moonlight to make sure they were still intact. There was some uncanny beauty in them, and in my arms in the blue light. I brushed my fingers against my collarbone, covered with my warm, soft skin. My hand glided downwards, underneath my shirt, meandering along the curves of my breast, waist and hip.

Take a step backwards, bring it back; and forward again...

No wonder dance was such an important part of religious rituals in so many cultures. It was magic of the body and the ultimate celebration of the life in it – a defiance against death. The beat of Obaachan's Latin songs started in my head and grew louder, till it became a battle drum; and I was ready to face the night, armoured with youth and beauty. I turned and swayed, felt myself return to my body and settle in it.

I became aware of a pink glow in the distance. Then it occurred to me: it was Tokyo! Tokyo was alive in the night! And it always will be – someone will always be young. I inhaled deeply, and felt as if the sweet heavy air might burst my chest. My legs began moving, my arms spread out, life awakening again in them, inch by inch like an electric current. I swayed with the breeze, cicadas and trees in the symphony of night.

Let it burst! I will scatter into pieces, and let the wind carry me through the streets, right into the heart of that palpitating glow.

'What in the Lord's name are you doing?!' My mother's shrill whisper suddenly came from inside the room, making me jump. 'Are you crazy?! Skipping half-naked for all the neighbours to see. You're not a child anymore – cover yourself and come back to bed!'

So I did, having befriended the night.

Dream Boats

| ١ ١ (١(١١١ ١ ١١

Jane Roberts

Do we ever scrutinize the Modernist buildings of the cityscape? Look closer, when the moonlight washes over them. Glazed walls like the sheen of a metal hull; grand wrap-around casement windows; Art Deco motifs stacked upon concrete, funnelling off into the clouds; lofty railings built for passengers – oh, why is everyone asleep? – to scan the starry horizon. It is the balancing revolutions of our planet that anchors them static, paired with our dwindling imagination, that is blind to these majestic vessels passing each other, ever so stealthily, in the night.

(hippocampus paradoxus)

| | (|| ||| ||

Valentine Carter

The seahorse has anchored his tail around the stem of a plant. His pregnant belly is taut and translucent, so everything suspended inside is outlined. Even though his eyes seem bright and watchful, I sense he is asleep. His gills pulse as he drifts back and forth in the listless currents of his tank.

Her bedroom is only lit by the blue light of the aquarium at the head of the bed. Thick curtains drawn against the amber streetlights. Our bare skin is bleached bright; pale and unreal against the tangled sheets.

'Don't look,' she says, knowing I will.

I like that she is suddenly shy, careful of us. I turn my head away and, unable to resist the temptation, I watch her reflection in the glass of the tank. She steps into the harness and pulls it up over her thighs, frowning, adjusting as she goes. She tightens the straps, pulling the leather through the buckles so the bite is enough, secure. She runs her thumbs inside the thick bands as they run around and under her, testing, checking. She wraps her fingers around its narrow girth and grins. She is pleased, confident. I watch her standing there and it's as if, for a moment, some other presence has stepped into the room.

'You can look now,' she says.

I don't need to confess that I have seen everything.

She slides my glasses down my nose and unhooks them from behind my ears. Her green-grey eyes blur, disappearing into smudges of dark and pale. All the colours are altered by the light from the aquarium. She reaches to put the glasses somewhere safe as I blink to make the world comes into focus a little more. I feel more naked than I did only moments ago. Vulnerable. I can't tell how far or near or sharp or dull my surroundings are. Then the room is full of murmurs and sighs and all I am sure of is this kiss, these arms, my body reaching, the quickening of our breath, time loosening.

There comes a very clear instruction; two sure hands insisting I move over, turn this way, kneel there and then I am stilled, two steady palms flat on the bed, forehead almost against the tank, her knees resting inside my own, her feet against my arches. It is a promising architecture. She pushes into me.

When he wakes, he uprights himself and untangles his tail. More like a dragon than a horse, he puffs out his chest and his fins propel him across to a nub of coral. He seems patient, peaceful, in command of his little world. What he is expecting to happen, will happen. His pregnancy seems to make him more male, even though I can't tell the difference between the sexes. The seismic subtleties of his gender an irrelevant significance. His feminine side has mastered him. He sways in time with the reeds, at home.

She hesitates. It is like the edge of a precipice. A black blade in the blue night. We have talked about this. This moment. She pulls away, a little, then a little more, until nothing moves at all, not even the blood through my veins or the air in my lungs. I am stuck, wedged against this decision. I know I want this but I cannot say the words, form the sentence, hear it out loud. Even before, in the daylight, I had to write it down. It is not that I am ashamed. I am not. But I am afraid to be wrong about myself, that I will ruin some part of me that I have yet to discover.

'Yes?' she says, the word only a breath into my hair.

There is a certain force necessary, a force I expected. Anticipation directs it along my spine, winging my shoulder blades. The weight of it is bearable. But the pain – brief, but still – elongates along all these shallow nerves until the words I wouldn't use become meaningless to me. The small concerns seem so far away, belonging to a distant planet. Lightyears pass. Then, as she shifts, deeper, the pain lengthens all the way down to a heavy pleasure and I find myself on the other side of the glass.

There is a memory forming here. One I may carry with me forever. The possibility of regret is unbearable. I have a fear of spoiling us – I do – but the anxiety of ruining a part of myself is worse. I want to be right.

I reach out and put my hand on the tank. I'm not sure if I am steadying myself or reaching for comfort. The glass is cold and a tremor shivers through my fingertips which reaches down and down through my body. I put my cool hand on my hot throat and she stretches forwards, sliding her fingers between mine. I am caught. She slides her other arm underneath me, between my breasts, her fingers against my collar bone, her elbow against my ribs. I would like to solder myself into this place and time, fuse these points together like an archipelago strung out across an ocean.

When the seahorse gives birth his children will scatter, easy, like the seeds from a dandelion clock disturbed by a puff of wind. I would like to see that happen, to see whether he changes back to what I thought he was or whether he will stay as he is, content to drift in the current.

I can only let go. It is all I want now. I make the choice to make no choice, decide to let her decide. I beg her to take my voice from me and turn it into a sound I have never heard before. *Take care of this,* it says, *I would not give this to anyone, only you.*

Daylight Saving Time

| ١ ١ ١ ١١ ١١١١١١

Rebecca Rouillard

01:54. The mannequin in the window of River Island is watching me. I'm sure of it, even though she has no eyes. If she did they'd be looking in my direction. I'm sitting on a bench in the pedestrianised bit of the town centre in the dead of night and there's a mannequin spying on me. She's wearing this weird stripy shirt that only has a sleeve on one side. They say sleep deprivation can give you hallucinations, but I suspect the asymmetrical fashion disaster is real.

01:55. It's not even dark or anything. The street lamps are so bright it's like daytime. Daytime, but with a strange orangey-yellow glow. Saturday night, you'd think more people would be around. But it's just me. I look back at the River Island mannequin. Her elbows are facing forward in an unnatural way. *What are you doing here?* she seems to say. Like, if I weren't here, all the mannequins would be wandering round the shops together, trying on each other's clothes, bouncing on the beds in John Lewis, playing PlayStation in GAME. But because I'm here watching, they have to stay still with their elbows poking out the wrong way.

01:56. I hear a siren. It goes on for a minute and then fades away. I listen carefully and I can hear the siren again, but now I can't tell if it's in the distance or in my head, like an echo.

01:57. Here I am. Waiting for something. I don't even know what. I'm waiting for the absence of something. I'm waiting for *nothing at all* to happen.

01:58. Two minutes to go. They say loads of people thought the world was going to end at midnight on the 31st of December 1999. Even the ones who didn't believe it must have held their breath at that moment, waiting, just in case. I'm like those people. I don't believe anything is going to happen but I'm holding my breath anyway, just in case.

01:59. The more times I say it in my head, the more sinister it sounds: Daylight Saving Time. Like The Witching Hour. Daylight Saving Time. Like a black hole devouring the daylight. I'm on the brink, trapped in its powerful gravitation pull. I'm getting sucked in.

And then, I go back in time.

01:00. I knew it was going to happen but still it seems like a miracle. I am a time traveller. I make a small squeaking noise I would be embarrassed about if there was anyone nearby to hear it. I have goosebumps on my legs.

I look around me to see if anything has changed, to see if I can sense anything – if it feels different at all. The light seems slightly dimmer. Perhaps that's just my eyes adjusting.

But there's nothing. No difference. Of *course* there's nothing. I knew there would be nothing, but I'm still a tiny bit disappointed.

It's all Div's fault. Bloody Div. We were getting ready to go out. Friday night. Div was sticking her eyelashes on. Then she stuck her moustache on. It's her thing. *Gender is a construct,* she likes to say. This one curled up at each end. She poked me in the eye with the Dali one last week. At least this one had soft edges.

'You should just stick your eyelashes on your top lip,' I said. I can't wear eyelashes or moustaches. I have contact lenses – the eyelashes irritate my eyes.

And it would look weird if we *both* wore moustaches.

'We're going to be late,' I said.

'Time is a construct,' she said. 'What if time isn't a straight line? Imagine time is like this.' She took a strip of gum and folded it over.

'Time is a disgusting habit that leads to unhygienic littering?'

'No.' She grabbed a pencil and shoved it through the gum.

'I hope you're not going to eat that. You know – lead poisoning.'

'Pay attention,' she said, waving the impaled gum at me. 'What's the one time of the year when time actually bends?'

'I think time is bending right now.'

She ignored me. 'Daylight Saving. When the clocks go back. Aka 2am tomorrow night. It's like going back in time.'

'You're not *actually* going back in time, you know. It's just the clocks going back.'

'Yeah, but just for that one hour, it's like the *fabric of time* – our *concept* of time, at least – is getting folded back on itself.'

'What do you think is going to happen?'

'We're all made of matter. Matter is made up of particles, protons and neutrons. And protons and neutrons are made of *quarks*.'

'Quarks? Seriously?'

'It's true,' she said. 'When time is folded back on itself it's like we see the reverse of time – what's underneath. And what do you think is underneath? The opposite of matter is antimatter. And the opposite of a quark is an *antiquark*,' she announced triumphantly.

'You just made that up.'

'I did not!' she said, indignantly. 'Google it. Antiquarks are real. Anyway, in that extra hour when time folds back on itself you might catch a glimpse of a kind of reflection of yourself. A shadow made of antiquarks.'

'Like a ghost?'

'Ghosts don't exist,' she said. 'But then again, perhaps that's what ghosts are – just the residue of a person made up of antiquarks.'

'Complete bollocks,' I said.

'It's not! It's physics.'

'*Physics*. You don't know anything about physics. I think you got all this off *The Big Bang Theory*.'

She didn't deny it. 'So, I've got this idea.'

I hate it when she says that.

'*I'll* read that stupid space-pirate trilogy you're always on about...' she said.

I rolled my eyes. I've been trying to get her to read those books for two years. I lent them to her ages ago. 'And what do you want *me* to do?' I sighed.

'Tomorrow night, find somewhere to sit – somewhere public where there are usually crowds of people, in town. Wait for the clocks to go back and see if you notice anything weird.'

'Anything weird? You want me to go wandering around town in the middle of the night? You know it's Hallowe'en weekend – who knows what kind of freaks and weirdos could be out.'

'Hallowe'en is a construct,' she scoffed. 'It's no big deal – just an observation. Use your senses. It's like a science experiment.'

She always talks me into things. I'm like the girl in *Persuasion*. When we were eleven she got me to soak my hair in lemon juice and lie in the sun all day to see if it would go blond. It didn't. When we were twelve she made me poke a fork in the toaster to see if it would electrocute me. It did. I have got to learn to say no to Div.

'Fine,' I said. 'But you'd better start reading those books tomorrow. They're like a thousand pages each.'

'Can't wait,' she said, picking the top one off the pile and hitting me over the head with it.

01:01. So here I am. I just travelled back in time and now I'm sitting on a bench waiting for antiquarks. I wonder what an antiquark looks like. I imagine them as tiny dark creatures with razor-sharp teeth and huge devouring mouths. They'd be so small I wouldn't be able to see them anyway, but it's like when you look at a bedbug under the microscope and you can't sleep comfortably for weeks afterwards.

01:02. My skin starts itching like I'm getting bitten by mosquitoes. There's even a faint buzzing noise. I know it's in my head. It's all in my head.

01:03. I lift my eyebrow at the mannequin. There's a flicker of a reflection in the corner of the glass window. I whip my head around.

01:05. And then, just for a moment, I see them all. Like grainy CCTV footage, in fast-forward. The buskers. The shoppers. The chuggers. Buy and sell. Wheel and deal. Bait and switch. One step forward, two steps back. The crowds swarm and scatter.

Random clusters of particles gather and disperse. The dance of quark and antiquark. The relentless dance.

01:08. And then I get this feeling that I'm about to walk down the street and sit down on this very bench beside myself. A shadow version of me, made up of a million chomping, bloodsucking antiquarks. I look over my shoulder quickly, almost expecting myself to be already standing there. I shiver.

01:13. The mannequin is still watching me. There's a knowing look in her eyes. If she had any. I glance back at her and suddenly the window is a mirror and the *mannequin* is the antiquark shadow version of me. A thinner version, with questionable fashion sense, but somehow familiar – an essence of me left behind in this empty husk of a place. I can't tear my eyes away from her. If I look away for a second she'll move. The antiquarks will lose formation and attack.

01:21. Suddenly I feel conscious of all the particles in my body and I start to worry about what's tethering them. What if the string breaks, the thread snaps? What if they all just drift apart? What if *I* just disperse and float away? The silence starts to get really loud, a static roar. And over the top I can hear the siren again, in my head.

01:35. And now I can't move. I'm frozen. If I move I'll come apart. All my quarks will scatter. My shoulders, neck, scalp, have all turned to stone. I can't turn my head. I can't tell if it's just me or someone's actually holding me still. Squeezing me.

01:54. I take one quick breath in and the cold air cuts through. I stretch my neck, twist it from side to side. I exhale, slowly. The muscles in my shoulders relax. There's no one here.

I look at my phone. As I watch, 01:59 becomes 02:00.

Kikimora

| ιιιɩ ιιιɩιɩ

Sofija Ana Zovko

My grandmother used to tell me about her – the kikimora. She said she was a small creature living behind the stove, always causing trouble and over-salting her soup.

'The little devil,' my grandmother said, 'One day I will catch her, chop her up like a carrot and boil her in my soup. Then we'll see who's salty.'

I didn't believe my grandmother's threats. With her spotted arms and soft skin folding over like dough, she didn't seem to have it in her to boil a creature alive, no matter how many times I saw her wring a chicken's neck.

A kikimora was the easiest way for my grandmother to explain her growing forgetfulness. As her soups became saltier over time, her punishments for the troublemaker became more elaborate. 'I will crack her like an egg and roll her in batter, then toss her on hot oil and fry her like a schnitzel.' I got used to the salty flavour of my grandmother's soup, the way it soaked into the carrots and even made the metal of the spoon taste salty. We peeled the crust off the bread and mopped the salty soup out of our bowls. But the saltier her soup got, the thinner my grandmother became. Her body dried out like a fig. Her once-strong hands couldn't even chop an onion.

'Come here, Una, lend me your hands,' she said. Her fingers trembled as she wrapped my hand around the knife's hilt. She sat down at the kitchen table to put on her gold rings, which over time had moved from ring finger to thumb.

'My Una, you'd better learn to cook quick, or you'll end up like me. It can't be like that – people will say I never fed you.'

I felt the tears gather in my eyes as I chopped the onion. 'There's time, Bako,' I said. 'You're too stubborn to go anywhere.'

'True. And if I went, who'd watch over you?'

On Friday, I got back from work and she was gone. Her soup, her stories, her threats. A loaf of half-raised dough was sitting on the kitchen counter. I plunged my hands into its soft belly, like a child.

I leafed through the Bible-thin pages of her cookbook, through stews, štrukle and sweets, trying to find her salty soup. I searched in the cupboards, in the oven, in the larder and there it was, buried at the bottom of the freezer, in a Tupperware wrapped in plastic bags. *Soup for Una* – I traced my fingers over her handwritten note. Even her handwriting had grown thin.

Undoing the rubber bands, I opened the plastic Tupperware and turned it upside-down over a big steel pot. The frozen soup fell in with a clang. I turned the stove on low and watched the blue flames lick the bottom of the pot. Something wasn't right. Was it the size of the pot, the strength of the flame? I looked at the empty seat at the kitchen table, asking it for help. The chequered tablecloth had faded where my grandmother opened her cookbook, day after day, studying it like it held a secret. Maybe she'd written something in the margin of a recipe, like a treasure for me to find.

I turned back to the stove and there she was – a kikimora.

'What the devil?'

No taller than a pepper grinder, the kikimora's

hands looked like chicken feet and she was using a toothpick to stir my grandmother's soup.

'What are you doing?' I shouted.

The creature fell off the edge of the pot, grabbing onto a handle to keep out of the flames. The big pot started to tilt. I jumped forward, but it was too late. The half-thawed soup spilled over the stove down the oven door, and onto the floor. The pot crashed to a halt halfway across the kitchen. I felt my knees give way and sunk to the floor in front of the mess floating on the tiles, the circles of carrots, strings of parsley. Sitting on a slice of celery root was the kikimora, wringing out a small red cloth.

'Look what you did!' I yelled, angry the way people get angry at animals, knowing they have no power to respond.

The kikimora cleared her throat. 'I think you'll notice this was of your own doing,' she said, tying the red cloth over her stalky ears.

My mouth fell open in shock.

'If you hadn't shouted, I wouldn't have fallen,' she continued.

'Y-you,' I stuttered, 'You were messing with the soup!'

'I was salting it. Didn't you want salty soup?' the kikimora asked.

'I—. You—. Well, now I have nothing.' I dropped my hands to the floor, and the soup splashed around me like shallow bathwater. 'Not even her soup.' The tears began to seep from my eyes. I wiped them away, but they kept falling. Chopped parsley leaves stuck to my cheeks.

'I would kindly ask you to stop crying. You're salting the soup,' said the kikimora, using her toothpick to steer her celery raft.

I looked at the creature, her face that stretched out in front of her in the shape of a flattened beak. She was so small I could have flicked her across the kitchen like a coin.

'Didn't you hear me? There is no soup!'

The kikimora looked at me and at the soup on the floor. 'Well, are you going to keep crying or are you going to make more soup? I'm hungry,' She fished out a piece of chicken skin and slurped it up.

'I can't. I don't remember how.' A fresh batch of sobs burst out of my chest. An itching on my thigh interrupted my crying. The kikimora was poking me with her toothpick.

'Pull. Yourself. Together.'

'Ow, stop that.'

I pushed her away with a brush of my hand. She tumbled and fell.

'Ah,' she said, getting up, 'so you're that kind. The giving up kind.'

I wanted to grab the kikimora by the feet and grate her like nutmeg. She picked up her green and white skirts and made her way across the sea of vegetables, stepping from parsnip to celery, to onion, until she was out of my reach.

'It would make your grandmother proud, wouldn't it?' The kikimora looked at me with her apple-seed eyes, leaning on her toothpick.

It was pouring outside. I was standing at the bus stop, in the pitch dark. The streetlamp next to me flickered on every couple of minutes only to die out with a whizzing sound. The rain slid down my nose. I stepped back as far as the fence would let me, trying to get shelter from the branches of a chestnut tree.

'I told you we would need an umbrella,' said the kikimora, tucking herself deeper under my coat's lapel.

'It's not my fault someone stole it at work.'

'Full of excuses.' The kikimora continued to grumble while I stared at the bend in the road waiting for the bus to arrive. Its blurry lights appeared, and the bus came to a halt sending a splash of water onto the curb. The doors opened, and the driver looked me up and down as I brought the rain onto his bus.

'One ticket please.' I felt the kikimora poke my rib with her toothpick. 'Ow, I mean two please,' I said, handing the driver two coins.

He looked at me in my father's old coat, searching it for the second passenger. He gave up and handed me two tickets, raising his eyebrows as I stamped them both in the orange machine.

The bus jolted forward, and I swung into a free seat.

'A bus ticket? Really?' I said. 'You're smaller than a cabbage.'

The kikimora closed herself into the inside pocket and refused to come out. I tickled the pocket, but the kikimora chewed through the lining and hid deeper in the coat. It wasn't until I was walking through the supermarket, basket in hand, about to reach for a red onion that she reappeared. She clambered through my sleeve and smacked my hand.

'Red onions! Do you know nothing? That one,' she said, piercing a yellow onion like it was a deadly beast and her toothpick a sabre.

One onion, one parsnip, one celery root, one parsley root with leaves and six carrots later, I was in front of the meat counter trying to get the kikimora out from behind the glass. She was lifting the wings and inspecting the legs of the dead chickens behind the shop worker's back.

'Fat, lazy chickens that haven't seen a day of running,' she said, flipping the chicken over to squeeze its thigh.

'Sorry, what did you say?' asked the shop worker turning around.

'Those look like good chickens,' I said pointing to the ones getting roasted on a spit on the wall. While the woman turned to look at the spit, the kikimora dragged the smallest chicken to the counter and plopped it on the scales.

'Ah you know, it's easier sometimes to get it already cooked. Can I get you one?' asked the shop worker.

'Just that raw one, on the scales,' I said, searching the glass display for the kikimora.

'Oh, you already told me, didn't you? At this hour, I feel like it's been three days since the morning,' said the shop worker, wrapping the chicken's goose-bumped skin in red plastic film.

'There's no end to it,' I said and took the chicken from her, placing it in the basket.

She smiled at me and went back to carving a leg of ham.

I moved slowly along the counter, past wheels of Pag and Livno cheese, trying to spot the kikimora. She was next to a tub of pickled peppers, fishing them out one by one with her toothpick. I watched as she opened her mouth wide like a crocodile and swallowed a red pepper whole.

'You little devil!' I whispered.

'Oh, just one more,' she said, smacking her lips as she reached for another pepper. 'They're so delicious.'

'Unbelievable!' I walked off towards the cashier.

'Wait, wait, don't leave me,' she called after me.

I waited for the kikimora under the shop's awning as she dragged herself out, slowed down by the fifteen peppers she had vacuumed up.

'Unbelievable,' I said, as we settled into the back seat of the bus. 'You should be ashamed of yourself.'

'What? It was just a few peppers.' She licked her hands, getting the last drops of pickle juice. 'You know, peppers, they have to be good from the start if they're going to be good pickled. Red or white, it doesn't matter. But they need to be new and firm before you cook them. It's always good to add a bit of sugar. And of course, salt…'

She talked all the way up the hill, but I stopped listening after the third stop.

The kikimora balanced on top of my grandmother's three gold rings as I sliced a carrot into circles.

'That's too thin,' she said. 'It's not cabbage.'

'Who asked you?' I said and pushed the knife further to the carrot's end, slicing even thinner circles.

She commented on each chunk of celery before I added it to the pot.

'Too thick, too big. You call that peeled? That celery has enough roots to grow out of the pot.'

'Go away, you pest.'

I reached for the bag of salt, took a pinch and added it to the soup. The kikimora cackled at me from the granite countertop, sitting on another bag.

'What did you do now?'

I licked the fine grains stuck to my fingers – it was sugar, not salt.

'You kikimora! Damn you!'

The kikimora darted behind the stove taking the salt with her. I tried to grab her, but each time I caught her she slipped out of my hand like soap.

'I'll be doing the salting,' said the kikimora, standing on the ceiling lamp. She pried the bag of salt open with her toothpick and started throwing handfuls of salt at the pot. The salt fell everywhere: onto the countertops, the floor, into the soup.

'You're a nightmare! I give up,' I said, sitting down in my grandmother's chair. I felt the weight of the day pulling my bones closer to the ground. I leafed through the pages of the cookbook while the kikimora dug through the larder – moving, lifting, and turning cans and jars on a hunt for more pickled peppers.

Somewhere between the kikimora saying 'pickles again' and trying to decipher my grandmother's notes on the *right* way to make fritule, I fell asleep.

I woke up with my head on the kitchen table, my eyes still swollen from tears. The morning light was peeking through the windows. I wiped the gunk from my eyes as I walked into the kitchen. On the stove sat a pot of my grandmother's salty soup. I heard a sound from the stove and looked behind the pot, thinking I would see a red shawl and green skirt, but there was nothing there. Just a toothpick left leaning against a bag of salt.

dream lovers

| \ (((((((((

John Kitchen

Greg and Sal didn't get on. They avoided each other, but one year their dreaded Christmas dos coincided at The Dirty Duck. Greg bought Sal a crème de menthe. Conversation soon flagged, one thinking what to say next, the other talking about avocados, until Sal mentioned a dream she'd had recently. Something to do with a red balloon, a crazed snowman and buttercups. *Odd,* said Greg, **I've dreamt the same things, though not necessarily in that order.** Intrigued, they found a quieter corner and talked dreams. They regarded each other in a new light. Their dreams were so similar. They were dreamsharers. They laughed, expressed their amazement. Then their knees touched under the table. *We should keep dream diaries and meet up to compare. If we slept side by side, would our waking be synchronised? I'm game if you are, but no touching.* Greg slept in a sleeping bag by Sal's bed. They always woke together and compared their nightly adventures. Until the anteater nightmare and they really did need to soothe each other.

Even This Helps

| ι ιι ιιιιιι

Zoë Wells

It was 3am when I closed my laptop and realised that I hadn't eaten since that morning.

It wasn't that I felt the hunger – there was no dull ache, no physical reminder – but rather it occurred to me that I hadn't spoken to anyone since Phil that morning when he'd asked me how I'd slept, and I'd slept fine, and he'd slept fine, and he had to go to work now so have a good day and I'd gone back to my room and that had been that. So I must be hungry, but there was nothing left to eat except too-hard bread and too-soft fruit. And cornflakes. But I'd had that for breakfast, and dinner the day before, so I threw my old yellow raincoat over my pyjamas and headed on out to Tesco.

There's a certain thrill to being awake, specifically awake and about, at 3am on a Tuesday. It's not a time you should be up. It's an hour and a half away from the keenest joggers and smoothie makers, but it's late enough that even those forced night owls, the students and bar workers, are heading in for the night. The world is at its most silent at 3am – even the insects, birds, and rabbits seem to have quietened for a moment, as though they've nothing to run from, nothing to worry about, because the rest of us have retracted our claws and gone to sleep for now. Only the elements are in motion. The wind ruffles the leaves of nearby trees, and if you take a moment, stand still and look straight up, you can track the movement of the clouds by the stationary stars. Stand too long and you may start to wonder if the stars, too, might be moving. If the clouds are staring up at them as they shuffle quietly across the cosmos.

But the night feels so far away. I think that if I were to lay back on the grass and push my arms up into the sky, I could almost reach the bottom layer of clouds, or maybe the edge of the atmosphere. And if I stretched, put out my index finger and focused my whole mind on it, I might be able to prod the moon a little, push it further away and watch as the ocean tides ebbed and flowed to a stop as my titan hand pushed further into the dark.

Even at that, I'd never reach the stars.

The bush next to me rustles. Two spots of yellow light reflect back. These stars creep closer, blink, then duck and hop over the boundary between us. A black cat, her fur seeming to shimmer as it breaks up the light from the lamppost, looks up towards me. Ancestral night trapped in a physical, adorable form.

I offer her my hand. She regards it. Sniffs it. Pushes her face towards it. I ruffle her ears and she backs up a little, then moves towards me, touching my ankles gently as she walks past me, then swings back round and pushes her head yet again. Ruffle. She purrs, and the dance is complete.

'What's your name then?' I say, scruffing her neck, but there's no collar. She's a scrawny thing too.

'That's fine, then.'

I always wanted to get a big black cat called Sue, after the Japanese susuwatari, the soot sprites in Miyazaki films that scuttle under floorboards or in lofts. Fist-sized black balls that stare at you with those white-circle-black-dotted cartoon eyes as they wait for you to move, to announce yourself as some kind of danger. *Susuwatari, susu,* a sound that's gentle on the ears of a cat on some deep-rooted, innate level.

Giving an animal a middle-aged white name has a strange deliciousness to it too. 'Deborah, heel.' 'Here Bill.' 'Jonathan, sit.'

'You doing okay, Sue?' I ask.

She looks up at me as if to say 'do I fucking look okay?' while she grooms her skinny body. Her fur is matted along her chest, the white of her roots showing through the filth. But with a cock of her head it turns from 'do I fucking look okay?' to a 'darling, I'm always okay'.

My stomach grumbles. 'I'll be right back,' I tell her, standing up, and she paces behind me because she's a cat. Of course she doesn't understand. 'Just wait here, just wait,' but she won't wait, until I cross the road and I'm in the car park and she sits there, her sun eyes boring into me, and I hunch over against the wind and walk through those huge sliding doors.

The only lady at the checkout asks me how I'm doing as she scans through my £1 pizza and £3-worth of cat food. Her name is Deborah but she's not a cat. She doesn't have night or stars in her gaze, her skin, her face. She just has sleep packed in bags beneath her eyes.

'Not bad,' I say. 'Slow night?'

'The slowest.'

I nod in appreciation. She bags my items but forgets to charge me the extra 5p.

Outside I look for Sue, but she's already gone – back to the wildness to hunt for rodents, hopping from bush to bush, living out an adventure night after night. Or else returned home, tapping against a glass door, waiting until morning to be let back in.

I look back to that same spinning, ever-moving sky. Even this, even now, when there's nothing but me and the great nothing, the world feels almost too much. Too busy. Too rushed. But as a single distant car fades into silence, and the whole night falls quiet, you can hear the low hum of the universe return as a distant, distinct purr.

ABOUT THE EDITOR

Yen-Yen Lu is a freelance editor and writer. Her short stories have been published in online zines and the anthology *In Which Dragons Are Real But* (Fincham Press, 2018). As an editor, she is passionate about promoting underrepresented voices in independent publishing. She studied Creative Writing at the University of Roehampton. Her favourite things about the night-time are the lack of crowds, and sleeping.

ABOUT THE WRITERS

Valentine Carter has short fiction published by *The Fiction Pool*, *Bandit Fiction*, *In Yer Ear* and *The Mechanics' Institute Review* (Issue 15 and Issue 16), and poetry published by *Perverse* and *Visual Verse*. Her debut novel, *These Great Athenians*, published by Twenty Seven, has been shortlisted for the Polari First Book Prize 2022. She is studying for a PhD at Birkbeck, University of London

John Kitchen was a primary headteacher. After retirement he took a chance and signed up for a series of poetry workshops. He discovered he could write.

It was life changing. Now he enjoys writing poems, plays, short stories; sharing these with a wide range of audiences; and the great thrill of seeing his work in print.

Winifred Mok is a filmmaker and podcaster (*Kin: Fallen Star, Project FIA goes PC*) with a passion for stories, books and site-specific theatre. She studied English Literature and Theatre Arts at the University of Birmingham. She likes exploring the spaces of language, culture and identity, and spends most of her time reading, learning, making, and wondering.

Leanne Radojkovich is the author of short story collections *Hailman* (2021) and *First fox* (2017), both published by The Emma Press. Recently her stories have appeared in *Best Small Fictions 2021, Short Fiction Journal, Landfall* and *takahē*. She holds a Master of Creative Writing (First Class Honours) from AUT Auckland University of Technology. Leanne has Dalmatian heritage and was born in Aotearoa New Zealand. She now lives in Tāmaki Makaurau Auckland where she works as a librarian. 'Whose lounge?' was first published in the journal *Firewords Quarterly* (Issue 5, 2015). Website: leanneradojkovich.com / Twitter @linedealer

Angela Readman lives in Northumberland. Her stories have won the Mslexia competition, the Costa Story Award and the New Flash Fiction Review Prize. Her collection *Don't Try This at Home* was shortlisted in The Edge Hill Prize, and won The Rubery Book Award. In 2022 her second collection *The Girls are Pretty Crocodiles & Other Fairy Tales* was released. She also writes poetry. Her latest collection *Bunny Girls* is out with Nine Arches in November 2022.

Jane Roberts's fiction features in a variety of publications and presses, including: *100 Stories for Haiti, 100 Voices for 100 Years* (Unbound), Aberystwyth University, Arachne Press, *Flash: The International Short-Short Story Magazine, Litro, NFFD Anthologies, Refugees Welcome, Retreat West, Seventy2One, Stories for Homes,* The Emma Press, The Lonely Crowd, *The Mechanic's Institute Review, The Shadow Booth, Under The Radar* (Nine Arches Press), Unthank Books, *Wales Arts Review, Visual Verse* and Valley Press's *High Spirits: A Round of Drinking Stories* (Best Anthology, Saboteur Awards 2019). Website: janeehroberts.wordpress.com / Twitter: @JaneEHRoberts

Rebecca Rouillard has a Creative Writing degree from Birkbeck, University of London, and was the

Managing Editor of the Birkbeck Writers' Hub for four years. Her writing has appeared in various online and print anthologies, including *Watermarks: Writing by Lido Lovers* and *Wild Swimmers* (The Frogmore Press, 2017), *Dragons of the Prime: An Anthology of Poems about Dinosaurs* (The Emma Press, 2019), and *100 Voices* (Unbound, 2022) She was the winner of the 2017 Mslexia Novel Competition and works as a school librarian in South-West London.

Miyuki Tatsuma's writing has been published in digital and physical anthologies such as the *PAST, PRESENT, FUTURE* anthology by Forest Publications (Edinburgh), and *Bounds Green Book Writers' Lockdown Lit*. Imagination in Isolation (London). She grew up in Kraków, Poland, in a Japanese-Polish-Italian household. Since moving to the UK in 2021, she has occupied a realm between four cultures – an existential status which greatly informs not just her writing but also her personal ontology. Though she had written in prose since age ten, one fateful day she woke up and has only created poetry since.

Zoë Wells is a writer, poet and translator from Geneva, Switzerland, currently based in Manchester, UK. Her writing has been featured in a number of publications, including *STORGY, Poetry Wales, Bandit Fiction, Hypertrophic Press* and *Ink, Sweat and Tears*. She has previously been longlisted for the BBC National Short Story Award, the White Review Short Story Prize, and the Bridport Prize. She is currently drafting an AI-based grief fiction novel, as well as editing a collection of translated poems from the French-language writer Renée Vivien. Twitter: @zwells_writing / Website: zwells.com

Sofija Ana Zovko is a writer, editor, and translator from Zagreb, Croatia. She holds an MSt in Creative Writing from the University of Oxford, focusing on depictions of the Balkans. Her work can be found in *Ash, Flash Fiction Magazine* and *harana poetry,* and two of her stories were longlisted for the 2021 Mslexia Short Story Competition. You can find her on Twitter at: @sofijazovko

ABOUT THE EMMA PRESS

small press, big dreams

☙❧

The Emma Press is an independent publishing house based in the Jewellery Quarter, Birmingham, UK. It was founded in 2012 by Emma Dai'an Wright and specialises in poetry, short fiction and children's books.

The Emma Press has been shortlisted for the Michael Marks Award for Poetry Pamphlet Publishers in 2014, 2015, 2016, 2018 and 2020, winning in 2016. Moon Juice, a poetry collection by Kate Wakeling for children aged 8+, won the 2017 CLiPPA.

In 2020 The Emma Press received funding from Arts Council England's Elevate programme, developed to enhance the diversity of the arts and cultural sector by strengthening the resilience of diverse-led organisations.

The Emma Press is passionate about publishing literature which is welcoming and accessible.

Visit our website and find out more about our books here:

>Website: theemmapress.com
>Facebook @theemmapress
>Twitter @theemmapress
>Instagram @theemmapress